Around the ZOO with Baboon

by Meish Goldish
illustrated by Steve Jenkins

Harcourt

Orlando   Boston   Dallas   Chicago   San Diego

Visit *The Learning Site!*

www.harcourtschool.com

Baboon has come to the zoo. "This is your new home," the man at the zoo said.

Baboon sat quietly in her tree.
"This is a big zoo," she said.
"I think I'll see who is here."

Baboon swooped down from her tree. She climbed around and met Goose. "Good afternoon," said Baboon.

"Hello," said Goose. "Come in the pool and get cool. There's plenty of room."

Baboon climbed around the zoo
some more and met Peacock.
"Good afternoon," said Baboon.
"I like your feathers."

"Me, too," said Peacock. "My
feathers are so pretty. Your nose
is very pretty, too. It is the color
of fire."

Baboon climbed around the zoo some more and saw Rooster up on a roof. "Good afternoon," called Baboon.

"Cock-a-doodle-doo!" cried
Rooster. "You can sit on the
roof if you're careful."
"Maybe soon," said Baboon.

Baboon climbed around the zoo
some more and met Moose.
"Good afternoon," said Baboon.
"What's that on your head?"

"These are my antlers," said
Moose as he shook his head.
They look heavy, thought Baboon.

Baboon climbed around the zoo
some more and met Tiger. "Good
afternoon," said Baboon.

"Hi," said Tiger. "I'm going
to take a nap. Would you like
to take one, too?"
"Maybe next time," said Baboon.

Baboon climbed around the zoo some more and met Raccoon. "Good afternoon," said Baboon.

"Well, hello there," said Raccoon.
"The moon will come up soon.
You can snoop for food with me."

Baboon climbed back to her tree. She rested against it. "I like this zoo," she said. "I made so many friends today."

16